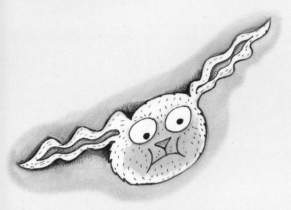

Carolrhoda Books
A division of Lerner Publishing Group, Inc.
241 First Avenue North
Minneapolis, MN 55401 USA

For reading levels and more information, look up this title at www.lernerbooks.com.

Main body text set in Coventry ITC Std.
Typeface provided by International Typeface Corp.

Library of Congress Cataloging-in-Publication Data

Carlson, Nancy L., author, illustrator.
    Sometimes you barf / written and illustrated by Nancy Carlson.
        pages   cm
    Summary: Although humans and animals everywhere vomit sometimes, it can be a scary experience when you are sick.
    ISBN 978–1–4677–1412–9 (lib. bdg. : alk. paper)
    ISBN 978–1–4677–4624–3 (eBook)
    [1. Vomiting—Fiction. 2. Sick—Fiction.] I. Title.
PZ7.C21665So 2014
[E]—dc23   2013048157

Manufactured in the United States of America
1 – DP – 7/15/14

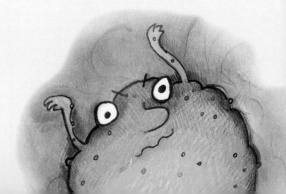

Sometimes You BARF

DISCARDED

NANCY CARLSON

Carolrhoda Books
MINNEAPOLIS

Dedicated to Hector
and Mrs. Paustian,
and you know why!!

—Love, Nancy

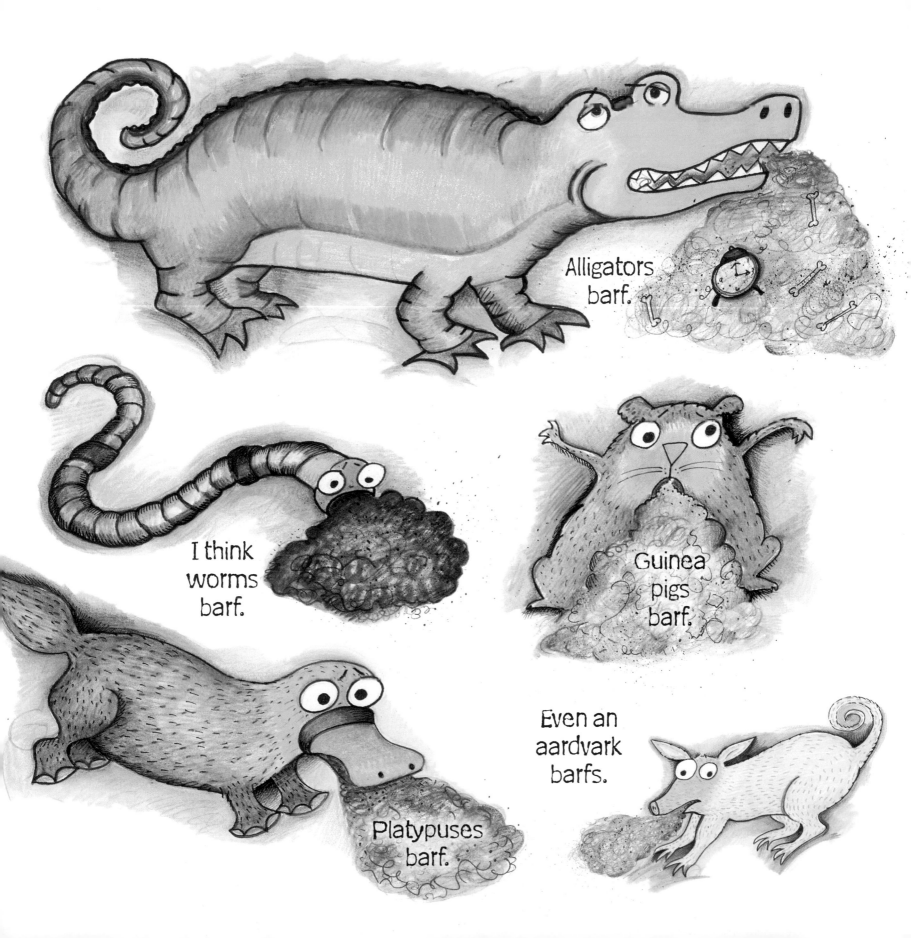

When a dog is going to **barf...**

Then you find things like one of your missing socks!

First, that icky flu bug finds you!

Then you don't quite feel right.
You start to feel queasy.

You feel kind of green!

Interesting Made-Up Fact!

When a lizard feels like barfing,

it turns pink!

When that flu bug finally picks you . . .

... at first you really try not to barf ...

The janitor will come with his special barf cleanup machine.

And you will find yourself sitting in the nurse's office holding a bucket and waiting for your mom.

Then your mom will
stick you in bed.

That flu bug will hang around for a while.

But soon, you can drink a little water,

nibble some crackers,

and then eat a bowl of soup.

But don't worry. No one will be mad at you for barfing . . .
except Nancy, who is still in her locker.

You have a great day, even though . . .

Here's the deal: Sometimes you barf...

But it's okay. You get better!

Right, Archie?
Archie? Archie . . . .